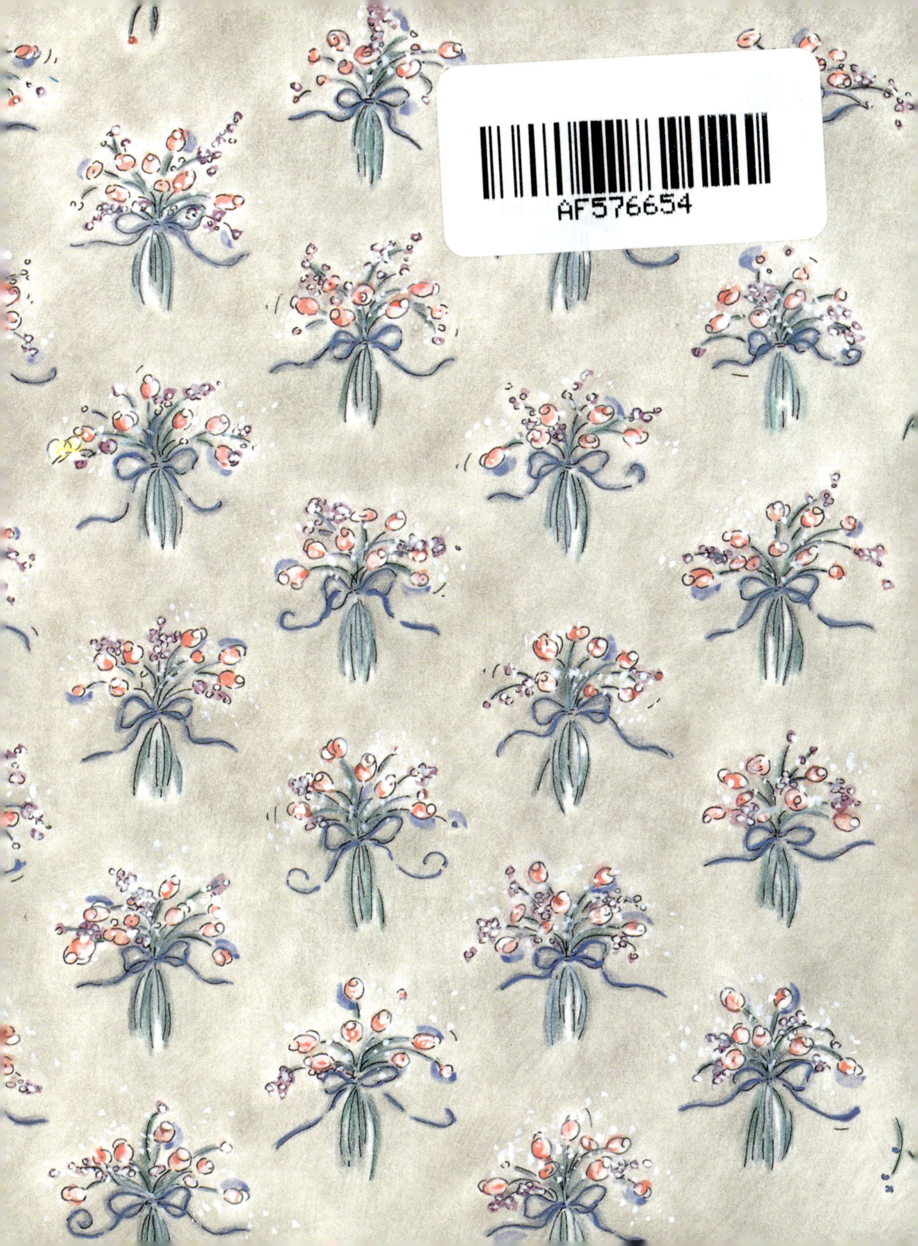
AF576654

With the very best of wishes

to Brett and Mike

from Mary Dowling

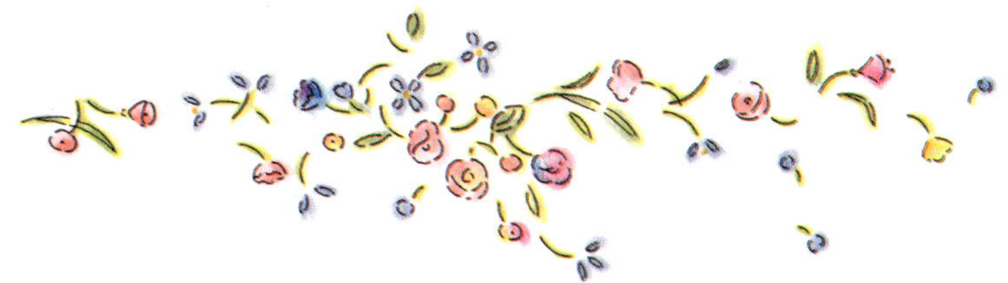

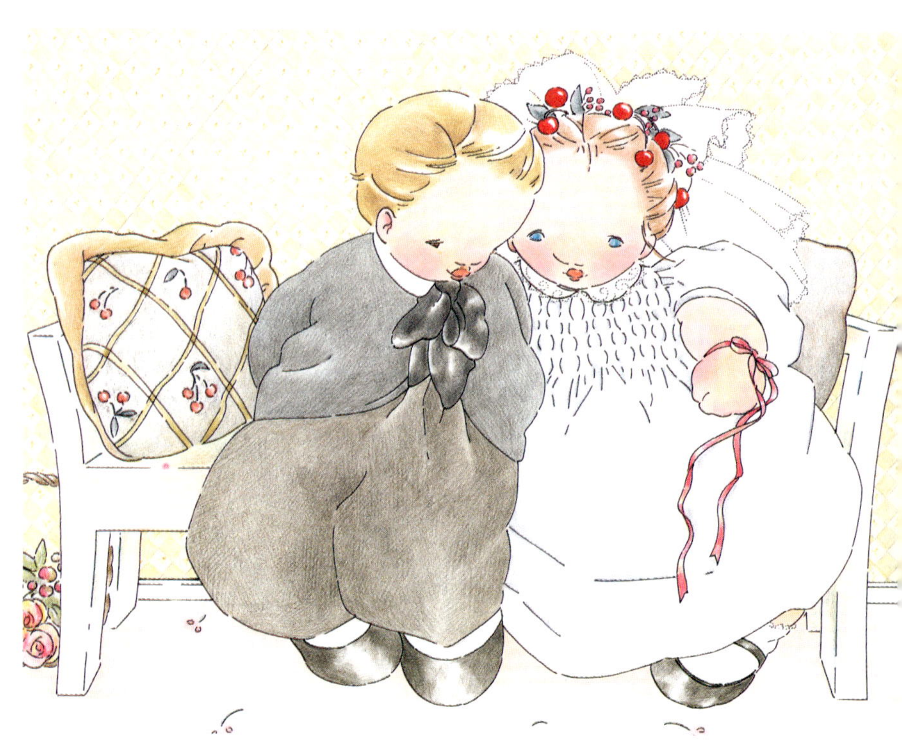

A Happy Ever After!

illustrated by
michel bernstein

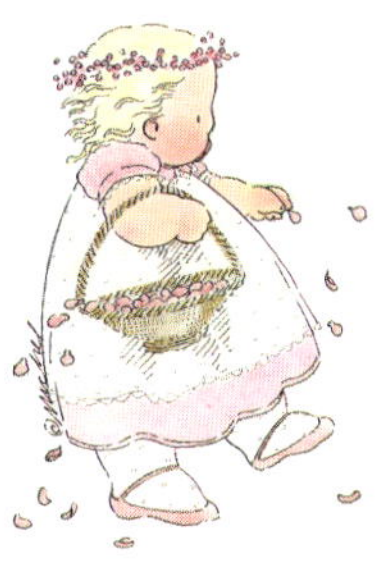

Andrews and McMeel
A Universal Press Syndicate Company
Kansas City

 Printed in Singapore. For information write Andrews and McMeel, a Universal Press Syndicate Company, 4900 Main Street, Kansas City, Missouri 64112.

ISBN: 0-8362-4714-0

A Happy Ever After!

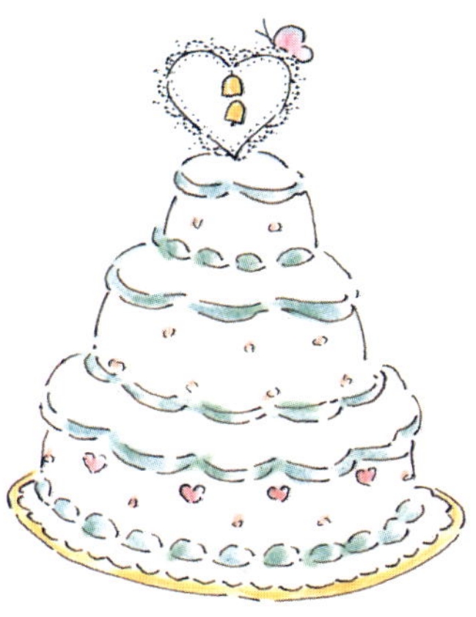

A happy ever after
is beginning
as you walk down the aisle
and say, "I do"...

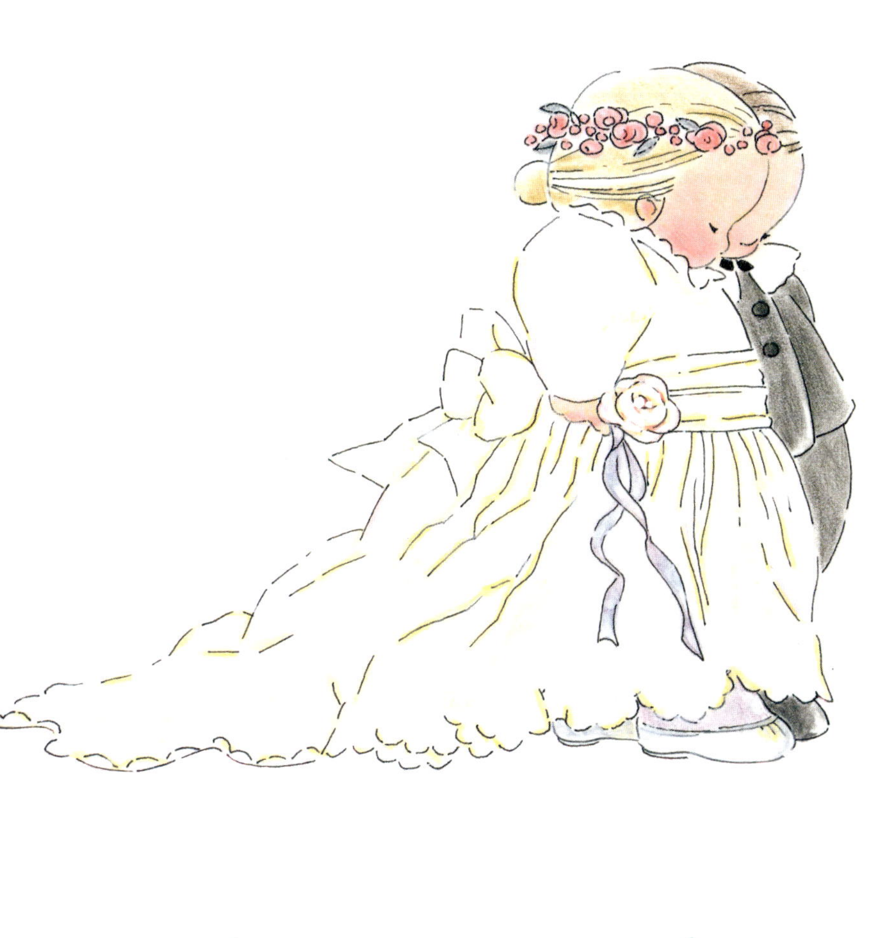

...a love that will bloom
lovelier each season...

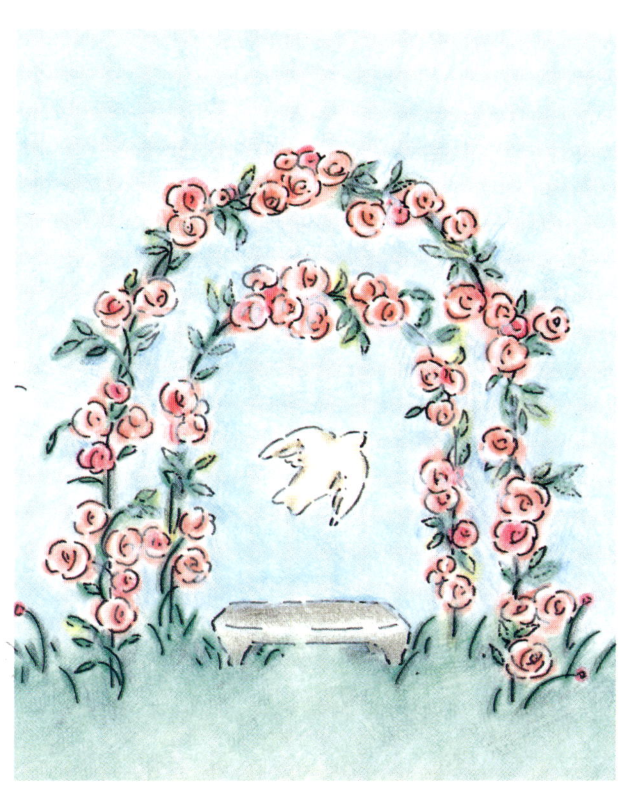

. . . a friendship
that will last
a lifetime through.

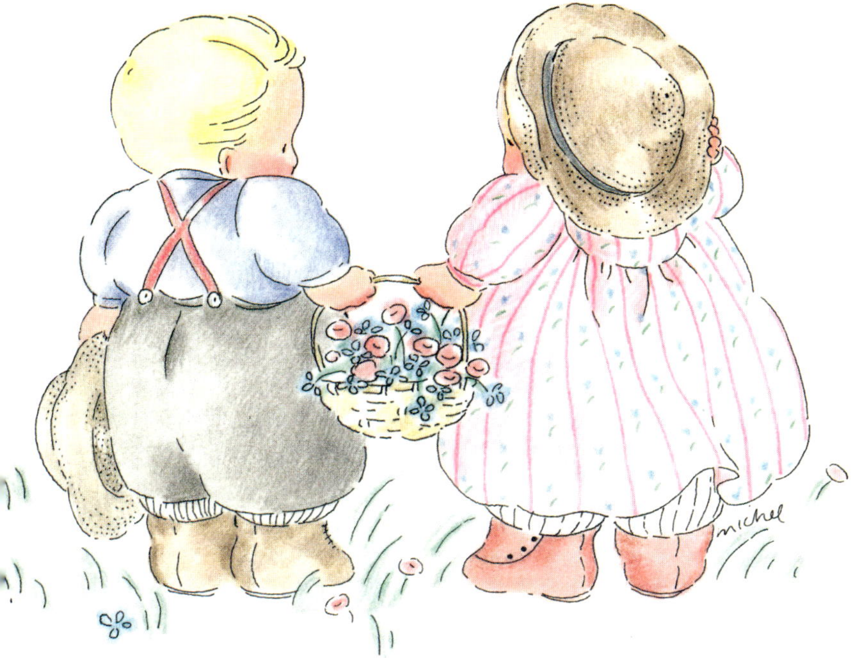

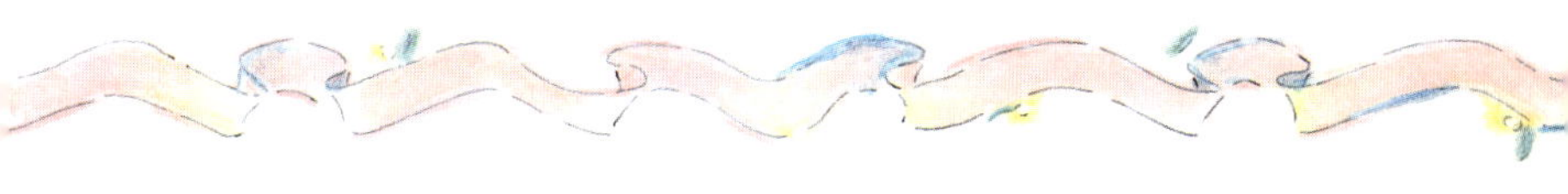

There'll be someone
to listen with excitement
whenever news is good
or days are great...

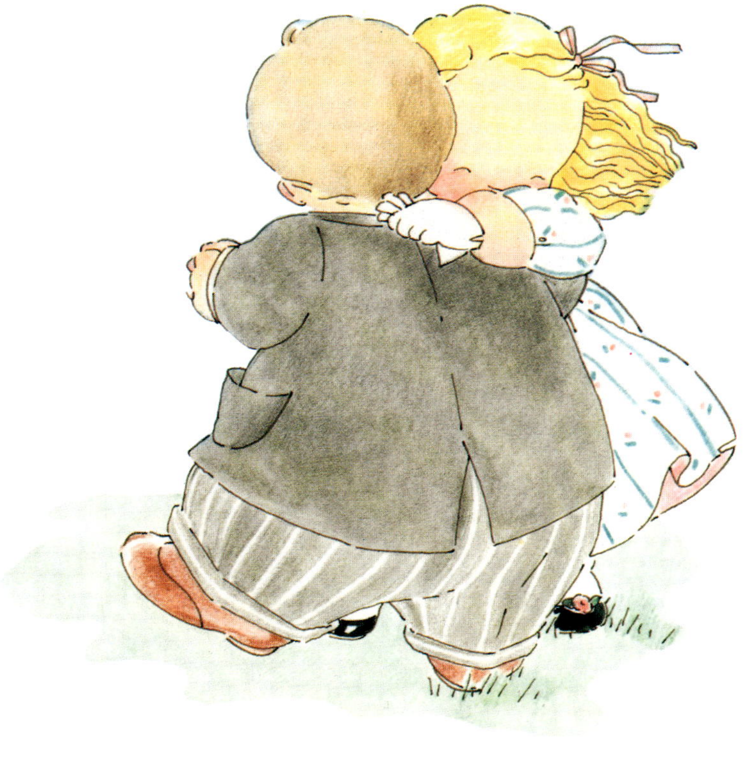

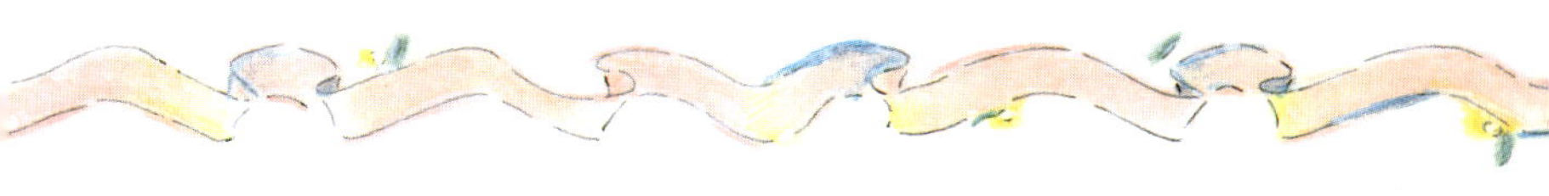

. . . somebody
who will make
the best times better. . .

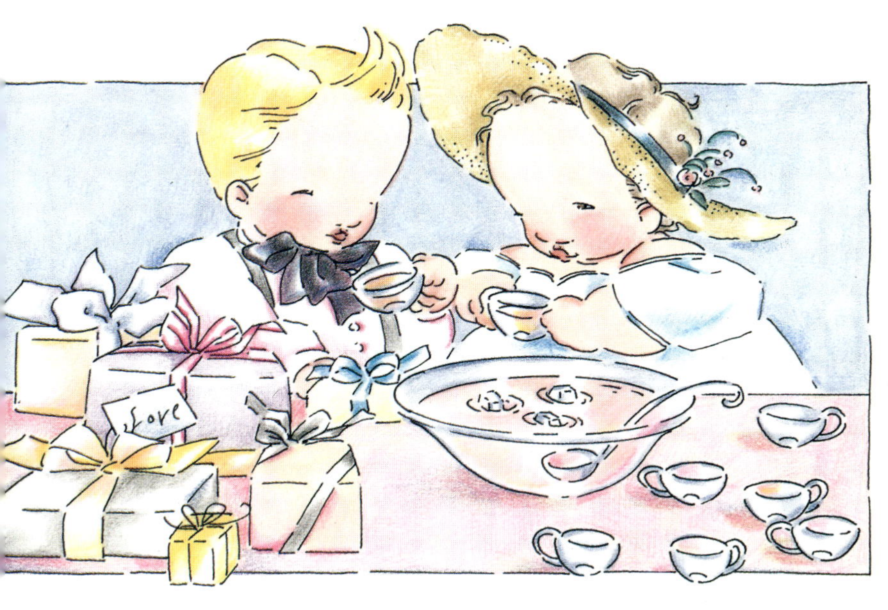
Love

...when you have
big events to celebrate!

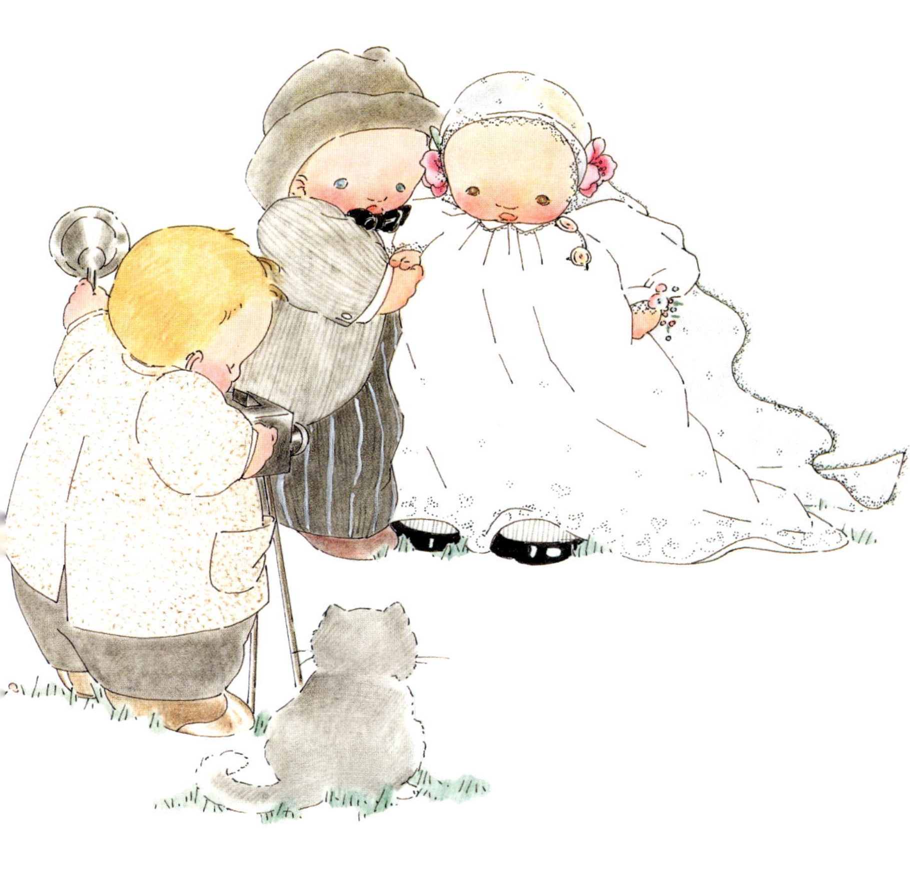

Encouragement
will be there
if it's needed...

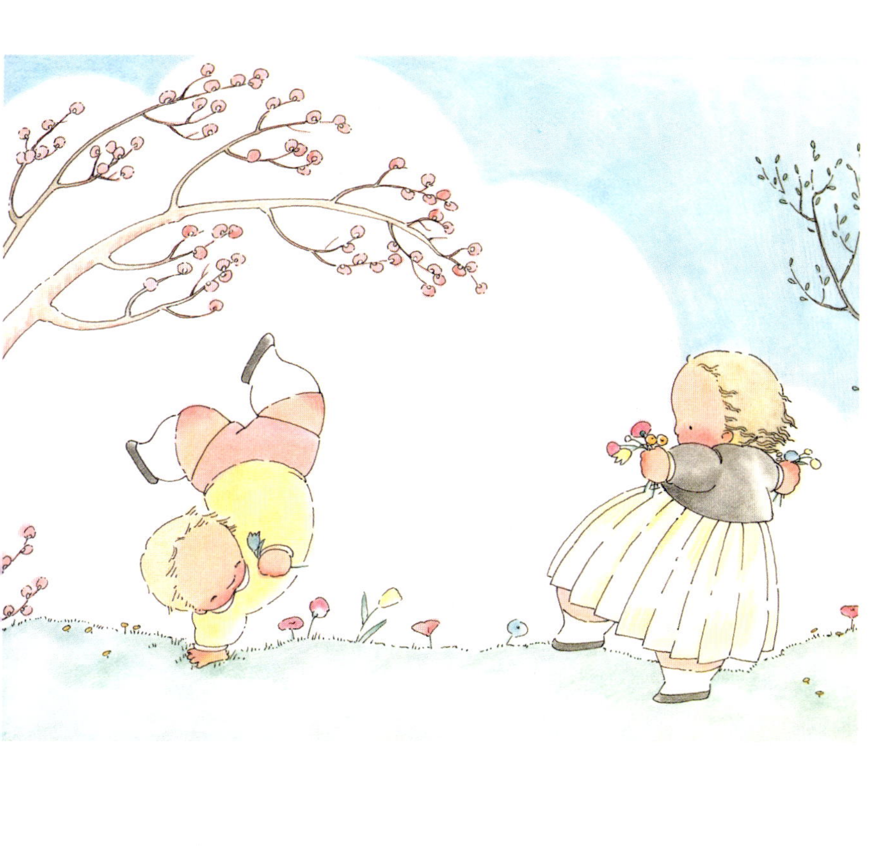

*. . . and laughter to help
chase the clouds away.*

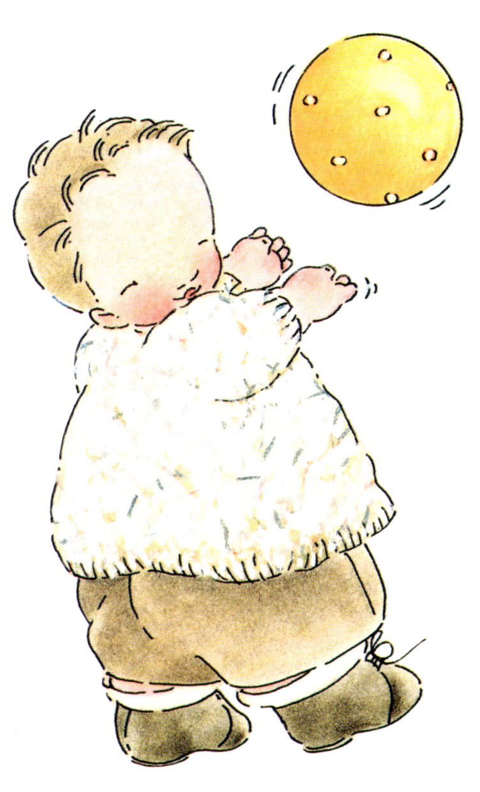

A tenderness
will warm
your quiet moments-

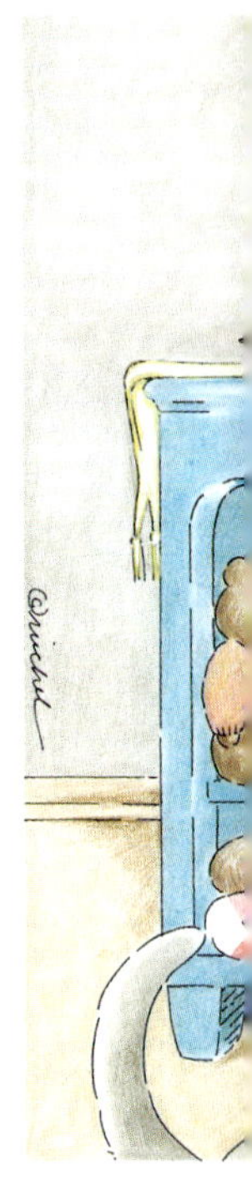

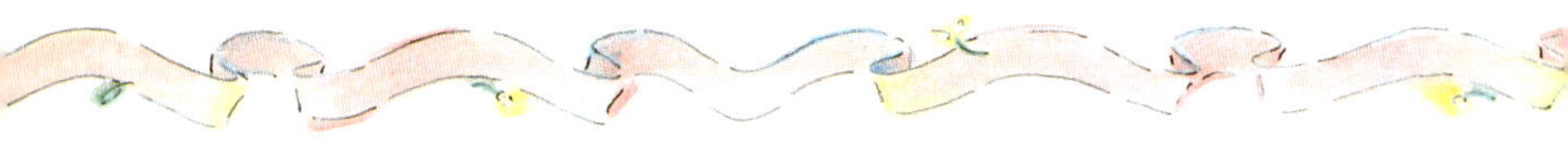

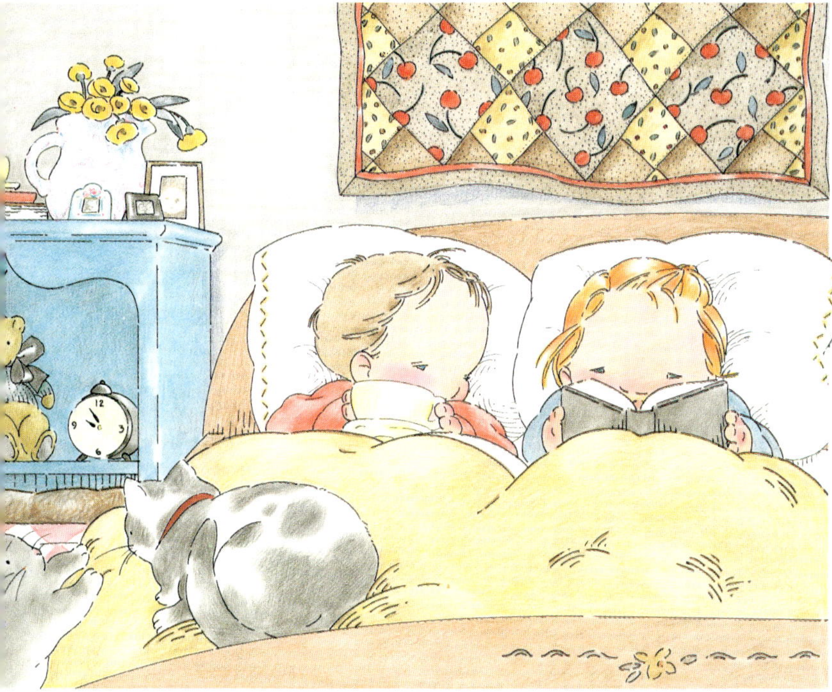

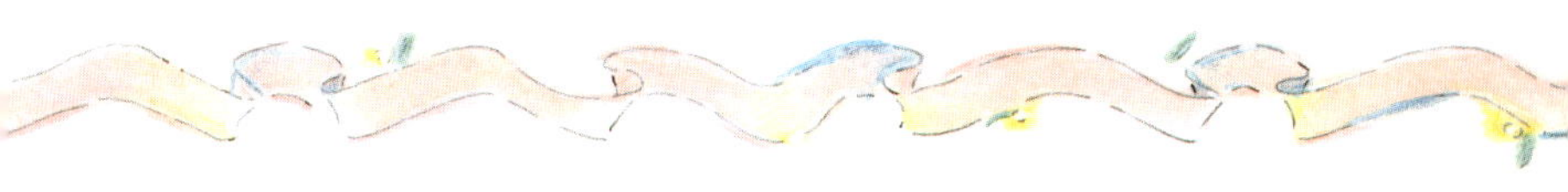

Devotion will
grow deeper
day by day.

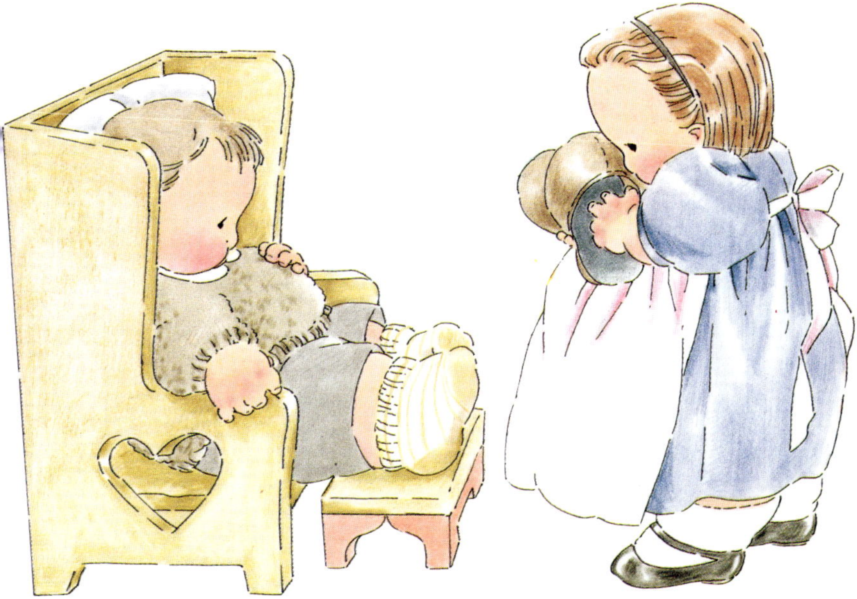

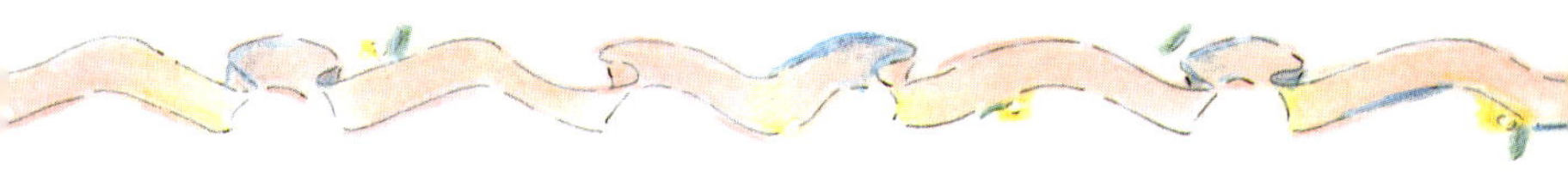

As every year becomes
a golden memory
and hopes and plans
turn into dreams
come true...

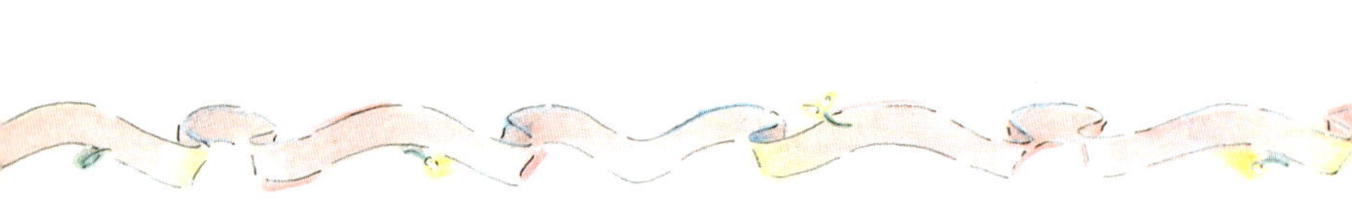

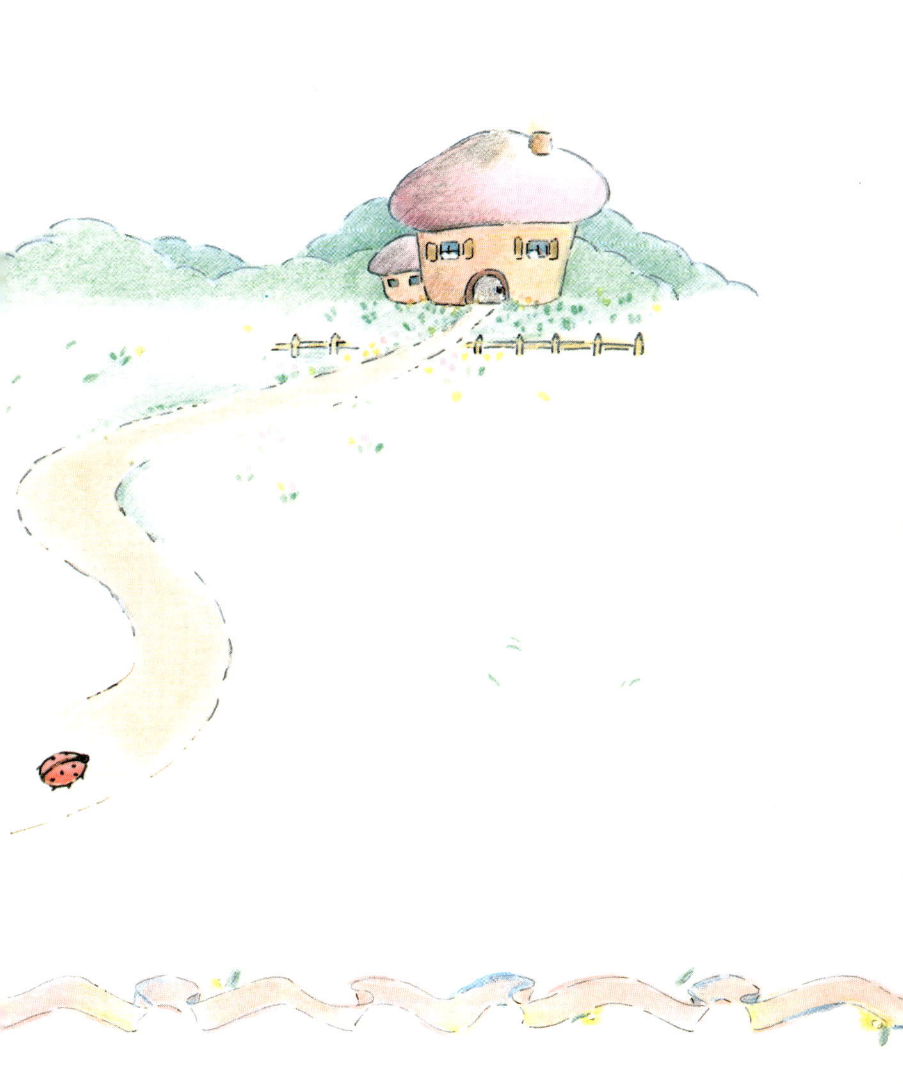

. . . may you look back upon
life's richest blessing-

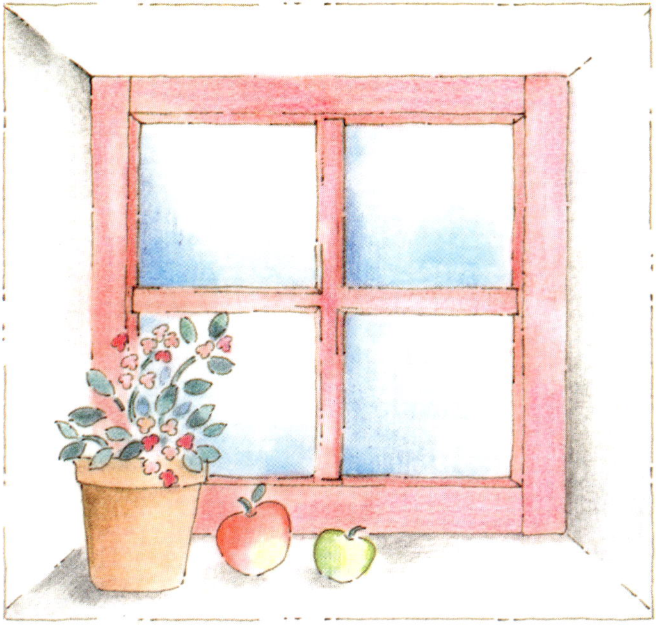

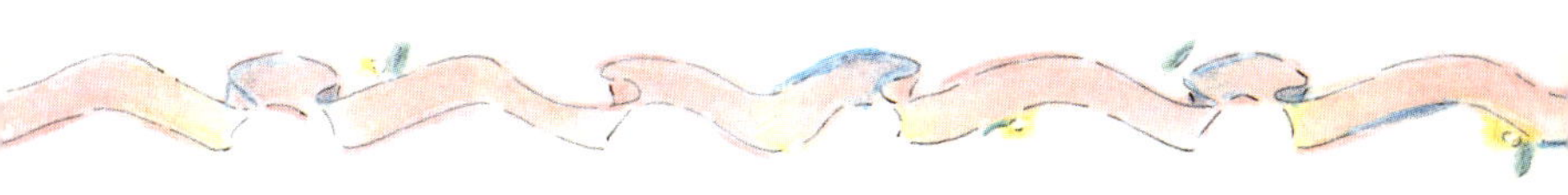

The happy
ever after...
meant for you.

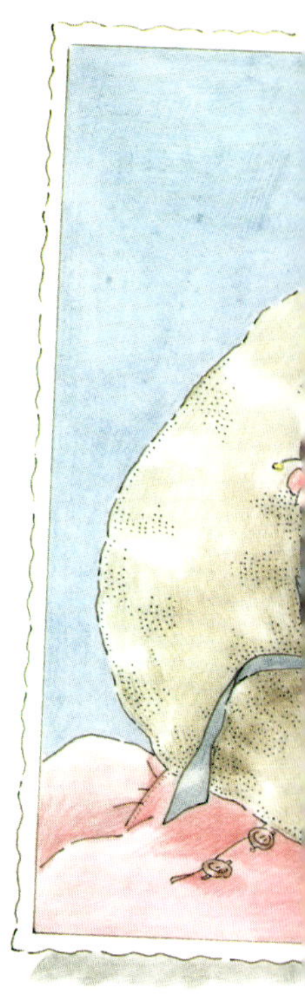

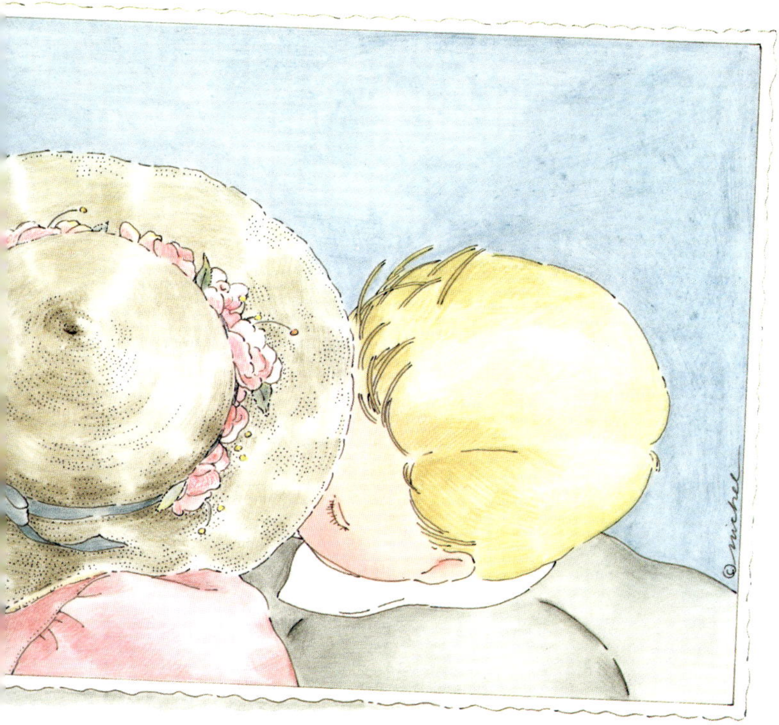

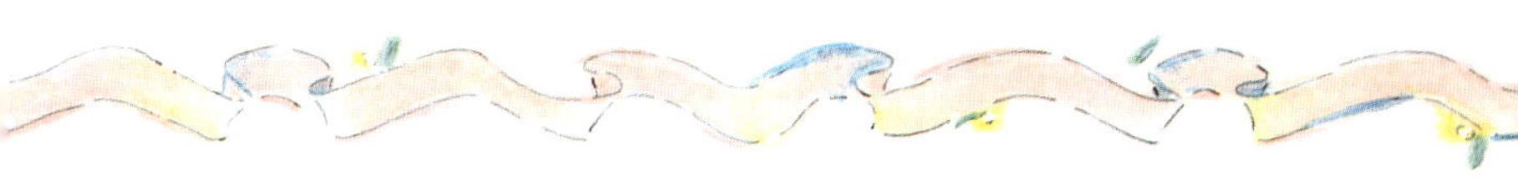

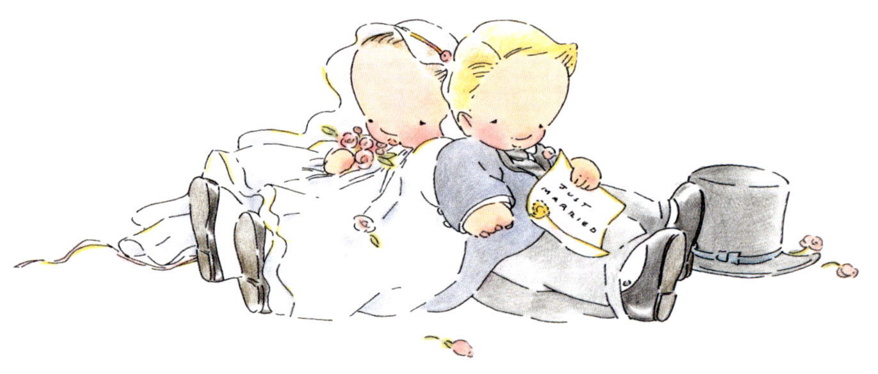
JUST
MARRIED

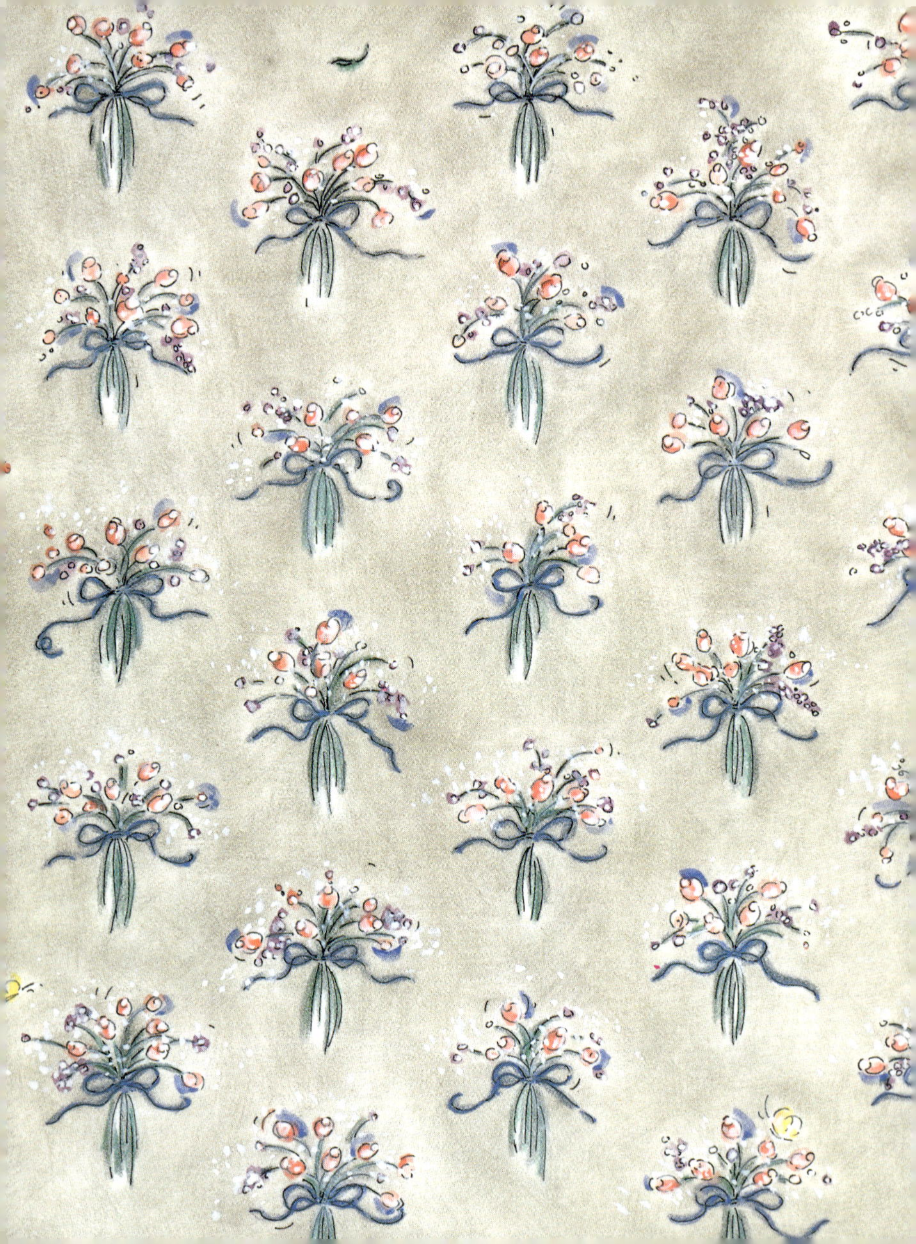